To Chris Moore, Myra Stephens,
and the whole Simmons family

Copyright © 1999 by Matt Novak.

For information address Hyperion Books for Children, 114 Fifth Avenue, New York, New York 10011-5690.

First Edition

1 3 5 7 9 10 8 6 4 2

Printed in Singapore.

Library of Congress Cataloging-in-Publication Data

Novak, Matt.

Jazzbo goes to school/Matt Novak.—1st ed.

p. cm.

Summary: Jazzbo does not want to go to school until he and his mother find just the right school for him.

ISBN 0-7868-0387-8 (trade: alk. paper)—ISBN 0-7868-2339-9 (lib: alk. paper)

[1. First day of school—Fiction. 2. Schools—Fiction. 3. Bears—Fiction.] I. Title.

PZ7.N867Jaz 1999   [E]—dc21 98-32070

JAZZBO
GOES TO SCHOOL

MATT NOVAK

HYPERION BOOKS FOR CHILDREN
NEW YORK

Jazzbo's momma said, "Today we are going shopping for a school for Jazzbo."

"I do not need a school," said Jazzbo.

"You will learn new things," Momma said.

"I already know things," said Jazzbo.

"This is my nose, and these are my toes."

"You will like school," said Momma.

"I will not," Jazzbo said.

"We will see," said Momma.

First they stopped at Grumpity School.
"We work all day," said the teacher.

"I do not like Grumpity School," said Jazzbo.

Next they stopped at Willy Nilly School.
"We play all day," said the teacher.

"I do not like Willy Nilly School," said Momma.

"I told you," said Jazzbo, "I do not need a school."

Then they came to Super School.

"Good morning," said the teacher.

"I am Miss Boggle. Welcome to Super School."

Jazzbo said, "I do not need a school."

"I see," said Miss Boggle, "but our school needs you."

"It does?" asked Jazzbo.

"Oh yes," said Miss Boggle.

"Weeza needs someone to play games with.

Skitter needs someone to read with."

"Googy needs someone to laugh with.

And I almost forgot someone," said Miss Boggle.

Then it was time to go.

"I hope to see you again," said Miss Boggle.

"I learned a lot today," said Jazzbo.
"You made friends, too," said Momma.

They both agreed that Super School
was just right for Jazzbo.

And they sang "ABC-123" all the way home.